TITLES AVAILABLE IN BUZZ BOOKS

THOMAS THE TANK ENGINE

1 Thomas in trouble
2 Toby and the Stout Gentleman
3 Percy runs away
4 Thomas and the Breakdown Train
5 Edward, Gordon and Henry
6 Thomas goes Fishing
7 Thomas down the Mine
8 James and the Troublesome Trucks
9 Gordon off the Rails
10 Thomas and Terence
11 James and the Tar Wagons
12 Thomas and Bertie
13 Thomas and the Trucks
14 Thomas's Christmas Party

FIREMAN SAM

1 Trevor's Trial Run
2 Norman's Spooky Night
3 A Bad Day for Dilys
4 Bella and the Bird's Nest
5 The Pride of Pontypandy
6 A Surprise for Sarah
7 Elvis's Experiment
8 Christmas in Pontypandy

TUGS

1 Kidnapped
2 Run Aground
3 Nothing to Declare
4 Treasure Hunt

BUGS BUNNY

1 Ali Baba Bunny
2 Knighty Knight Bugs
3 Broomstick Bunny
4 Mutiny on the Bunny

BARNEY

1 Barney and the Picnic
2 Barney's New Hair-Do
3 Barney Goes Shopping
4 Barney's Happy Christmas

MICRO MACHINES

1 Road Block
2 Hijack
3 Safe Breakers
4 Snowbound

GREMLINS

1 Don't Get Wet
2 Midnight Feast

First published 1990 by Buzz Books,
an imprint of the Octopus Publishing Group,
Michelin House, 81 Fulham Road, London, SW3 6RB

LONDON   MELBOURNE   AUCKLAND

ISBN 1 85591 022 5

Printed and bound in the UK by BPCC Paulton Books Ltd

Story by Fiona Hardwick
from the original screenplay
Illustrations by CLIC!

MIDNIGHT FEAST

buzz books

Billy Peltzer had been re-united with his
long lost friend Gizmo after he had rescued
him from an animal research lab.

Before he had had the chance to discover
what had been happening to Gizmo, Billy
had had to go to an important business
meeting, so he'd asked Kate, his girlfriend,
to take Gizmo home.

What neither Billy nor Kate realised was that Gizmo had got wet, and so had produced four new Mogwai. The new Mogwai had trapped Gizmo in Billy's office, and Kate had taken one of them home.

"That's not Gizmo!" said Billy, when he got back. "Where did you find *him*?"

"In the drawer, like you said!" said Kate.

Billy stared hard at Daffy, who tried to look cute. Then Billy looked at the kitchen clock. It was 11.15. "We have to get back to the Clamp Centre," said Billy.

"They mustn't eat after midnight. You know what that means . . ."

Kate shuddered as she remembered that night at Kingston Falls. They put Daffy into a bag and rushed off.

It was about midnight. The foyer of the Clamp Centre was busy. The assistant at the frozen yoghurt stand couldn't understand why the yoghurt was spilling so much. And the orders kept getting mixed up. Another angry customer appeared:

"This isn't what I ordered – ah! What's that? It's a rat!" screamed the woman as a furry paw grabbed some sweets.

Just then, Kate and Billy walked in.
"There's something furry in there," wailed
the woman. "It's horrible!"

Billy looked at his watch. It was 12.10.
"We're too late. It's after midnight, and
they've eaten. Now, they'll make cocoons,
and if they get into water . . ."

"Come on," said Kate.

A few minutes later, they were deep underground. "If we shut off the water supply, perhaps they'll close the building," said Billy, trying to open the enormous cage containing the machinery.

But Billy was being watched. Mr Forster, supervisor of the Systems Control Centre, called out his guards.

"Hands up! And what's in your bag, pal?"
asked one of the guards, watching the bag
with Daffy in it wriggle and squirm.

"Oh, nothing," said Billy, casually.
"Sure. Let's have a look. Aarrgh!!" Daffy
had grabbed hold of the guard's nose and
wouldn't let go. Eventually, he loosened his
grip and scampered off into the darkness.

Billy spent the rest of the night in a police cell. Kate got him released next morning and they sped over to the building. Meanwhile, Gizmo had escaped from the ventilator shaft where the Mogwai had trapped him. He landed with a squelchy thud on a heap of cocoons.

"Uh-oh!" he cried, as he was grabbed from behind by a green claw.

13

Billy went to the Systems Control Centre, where he met Mr Forster.

"What are you doing here, Peltzer?"

"Mr Forster, listen to me . . ." Billy explained about Mogwai and all the 'rules'. Mr Forster and his technicians didn't believe a word.

"I've never heard such a load of . . ."

Mr Forster's speech was cut short as two green arms burst out of the console in front of one of the technicians. Mohawk, now transformed into a fiendish Gremlin, grabbed the technician by the throat.

Billy turned a flashlight on Mohawk, and he let go of the technician. But it was too late. The Gremlins were back!

That morning, Microwave Marge was being filmed for the Clamp Cable TV Network. Suddenly all the lights went dim.

George and Lenny appeared on set. They put metal utensils in Marge's microwave ovens and turned them up to full power.

"Stop! Stop!" yelled the terrified Marge. The ovens exploded and caught fire, setting off the sprinkler system. Now there would be even more Gremlins!

Billy decided the time had come to talk to
Daniel Clamp himself. As he ran into the
room, he noticed that Mr Clamp's suit was
covered in Gremlin blood.

"They've been here already, then," said
Billy quietly. "They? You mean there's
more than one?" asked Mr Clamp. "I'm
afraid so. Sir, these things are dangerous.
We mustn't let them leave the building after
dark."

"How come you know so much about them, Bill?" Billy didn't know what to say, but then Mr Forster burst in. "We need some help sir. Peltzer, just what . . ."

"Seems like Bill here is the expert," said Mr Clamp, interrupting Forster. "We'll take him along. Let's get rid of these bugs before they can do any more harm."

On the eighteenth floor, Gremlins had broken into Splice-O-Life. "Not my vegetable extracts," pleaded one of the scientists. A Gremlin picked up the test-tube of green liquid, and drank it in one go. Then something remarkable happened.

All the other Gremlins followed suit, gobbling down Dr Catheter's experiments.

Poor Gizmo was down in the basement, being tortured by Lenny and George. They had ripped out the master lighting panel and were pushing Gizmo closer and closer to the live wires.

"Bil-lee!" cried Gizmo desperately.

By now, Daffy had taken control of the lift and was terrifying people by sending them hurtling up and down the lift shaft.

"Thank you for pushing the button," said Daffy, trying to sound like the lift's electronic voice.

Billy, Forster and Mr Clamp arrived at Splice-O-Life as a Gremlin was drinking the results of a lightning bolt experiment.

At first, it didn't change. Then, it disappeared into an electric socket, emerging a few seconds later, crackling as if it were made of pure electricity.

When the Electric Gremlin made a run at them, Billy held up a videophone receiver. The Gremlin dived into it, and Billy trapped him there, by putting him on hold.
Billy turned to Mr Clamp, who was looking desperate. "I've had an idea. Can you put all the clocks forward three hours? It could be the only way to save the city."

"'Developer Saves City' eh? I like that Bill. Carry on," said Mr Clamp.

"When the Gremlins think it's sunset, they will all go to the foyer and we can arrange a little surprise for them!"

As the clocks swept forward three hours, Billy remembered Kate. Where was she? He heard a scream.

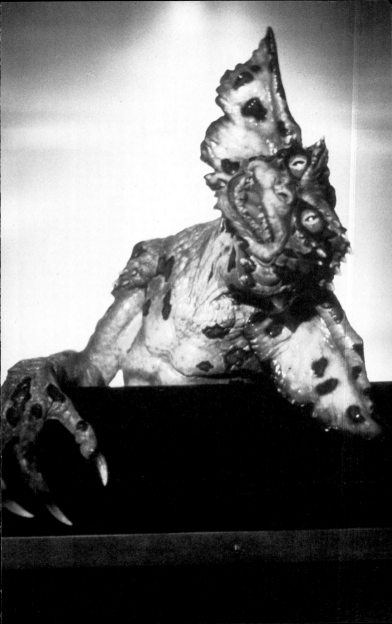

Nearby, Kate was cutting Marla free from a giant spider's web. Mohawk, who now had eight enormous spider's legs himself, was creeping up on them. He opened his ferocious jaws . . .

With a battle cry, Gizmo dropped on top of Mohawk. He threw a lighted match, and sent Mohawk up in flames.

Believing it was almost evening, Gremlins were gathering in the foyer, reading books like 'Dining After Midnight in New York'.

"Right, get that hose into position and turn it on," said Billy. "Put Gizmo in a box to make sure he keeps dry."

"But Billy, all that water – are you sure you know what you're doing?" said Kate.

The Gremlins were about to storm the doors when the hose was switched on. As they got wet, the Gremlins' skin started to bubble. More and more of them appeared, piling up in the foyer.

Billy handed Kate a videophone. "Can you transfer a call from the Systems Control Centre down here?"

". . . tap into the PBX . . . then the five digit code . . ." muttered Kate.

"That's it!" shouted Billy.

The Electric Gremlin had broken free. Billy held the receiver out over the flooded lobby. The Electric Gremlin shot out, and leaped into the water.

A massive wave of electricity ripped through the water, killing the Gremlins. Kate and Billy watched in silent horror as the foyer filled with green swampy mush, the remains of the Gremlins.

At that moment, Clamp and his combat troops arrived. While the troops cleared up, Mr Clamp stood and stared. He stared at the enormous building and he stared at the green mess in the foyer.

"Maybe I've got things wrong," he muttered. "What people want is somewhere quiet, like Kingston Falls. Do you reckon you could design a place like that, Billy?"

"Why sure, Mr Clamp," said Billy.

Gizmo twittered in his box. "What's he saying?" asked Mr Clamp.

"Oh, just that he hopes he can come and live with Kate and I now that Mr Wing isn't around," said Billy.

Kate turned round. "You can understand him this time, Billy – that means you're ready to take care of Gizmo!"

"Yes, I think I am," said Billy, smiling down at Gizmo.